My Ratchet Secret 2

Disclaimer:

D1506386

Seal The Deal

"So how much is this going to cost me?" I asked Dr. Johnson knowing full well that the price would be steep for what I required. I had successfully married the man of my dreams but it wasn't without a cost. I had lost my best friend in the process. I thought everything would be peaches and cream from here on out but now my husband wanted a damn baby, go figure. Oh well I have no choice but to do whatever I need to do to make my marriage work. I had tried my best to talk Adrian out of wanting kids so soon but he wasn't trying to hear it. In his mind he already had the perfect wife now all he needed was a mini me running around to make the story complete. I was able to please him in every other way but this is where I couldn't fall short. If this man wanted a baby I had to make it happen no matter what the cost. And if y'all think a bitch like me was gonna let the fact that I'm a man stop me and my boo from having our love child you got me all fucked up.

"I'm sure we can work something out," Dr. Johnson replied looking me over like I was a damn two piece and a biscuit from Popeye's, and he hadn't eaten in days.

Dr. Everest Johnson was recommended to me by a friend of a friend. He was a crooked Dr. to say the least. He ran a clinic on the far East side of town however besides his private practice he was also known for "doing favors on the side" such as writing prescriptions for narcotics for patients that didn't necessarily need them, and excuses for work related injuries for a cut of the lawsuit winnings just to name a few.

There was no limit to this nigga's hustle. Fuck an insurance plan. If you had the money Dr. Johnson delivered; be it in his office or at one of his many injection parties. For all you chicks that want a 23-inch waist and a 50 inch ass, Dr. Johnson was the man to see. He had the fat transfer, booty injection game on lock in the hood. A bitch could walk in looking like sponge bob square pants and leave looking like Buffy The Body. Personally I thought the shit looked ridiculous, these hoes walking around with twigs for legs and beach balls for ass cheeks, but to each his own. My shit was well proportion and that was all that mattered. It's a damn shame but I'm putting supposedly REAL women to shame with all this fineness.

What I would be using the doc for specifically would not only be to convince Adrian that I could not have children, but to suggest the idea of using a surrogate as well as hooking me up with a cute African American egg donor that would serve as my own. I couldn't use the surrogate's egg for the simple fact that she couldn't be in on the plot. All she needed to know what that she was to carry our child.

The plan was simple. Adrian's sperm would be used to fertilize the donor's egg, which he would think is mine and it would be placed in a surrogate for the incubation period. Dr. Johnson not only had a list of willing donors, he had their pictures as well, which was absolutely necessary because she had to be a bad bitch. I needed to make damn sure that my baby was cute. Booger bears need not apply.

I guess you could say that anything you wanted could be purchased in the hood as long as the price was right. There were plenty of young chicks trying to fund their college education and the money that came from being a handpicked donor was a pretty penny. This was yet another expense I was willing to dish out all in the name of love.

Judging by the way this bastard was looking at me I had a feeling that he wanted more than just money.

"I don't want to just work something out," I replied scornfully. "I want to know exactly how much this will cost me."

Dr. Johnson began to circle me like an animal circles its prey. "Damn you are sexy as hell," he announced as he ran his finger across my plump round ass as I was about to take a seat.

I quickly spun around and knocked his hand away. "What the fuck do you think you're doing? We ain't about to make THAT kind of deal."

At this point he just laughed at my attempt at trying to be hard.

"That's funny," he chuckled, "especially considering the fact that you need ME. Now like I was saying, I'm sure we can work something out."

This asshole was going to leave me no choice but to tell him I use to be a man. Maybe that would calm his horny ass down.

"Uhmm Dr. Johnson I need to tell you something, I don't usually put my business out in the street like this but seeing as you have your mind made up on how you THINK you are about to get paid, you should know that I use to be a man."

The Dr grinned and took a seat at the desk in his office.

"I know what you USE to be, but you are a woman now."

"*How the hell does he know I use to be a man?*" I thought as I subconsciously rubbed my chin, checking for any visible signs of stubble.

"Don't look so surprised, you think this is the first time I had to help out somebody like you in a situation like this?"

"What the hell you mean "like me"" I scoffed. The Dr's remarks totally caught me off guard. As far as I was concerned I was flawless as a woman. Shit I had fooled Adrian and droves of other men who shot flirtatious glances in my direction and tried to holla on a daily basis. What the hell was this bastard talking about?

"Yeah you look good," he responded, sensing my irritation and obvious discomfort at being found out. "However all the exfoliation in the world is not going to make those hands look any smaller. They are a dead giveaway."

"*Da fuck?*" I thought looking down at my hands. "*Do my knuckles look big? I wonder if they have a surgery for that?*" And all this time I thought my shit looked dainty. This was the first time since Tasha someone had actually called me out on being a man and I was none too pleased. I prided myself in looking like the softest, feminine woman a man could ever lay eyes on. Sure I had to stop Adrian a few times when I woke up to him caressing my damn face in the morning, just in case he felt that five o'clock shadow. Shit I had the hair follicles removed from my face but Dr. Yoon instructed me that I might have to follow up with electrolysis. This was yet another expense, plus I hadn't gotten around to it, seeing as my only priority at the moment was giving Adrian a baby.

As I sat in momentary shock from what had just transpired Dr. Johnson went on to tell me that he was in fact on the down low himself. He assured me that I was still fine to him.

"It ain't no big ooooh wee, I'll still hit. I've been wanting to try some tranny pussy anyway" he smirked while rubbing his hands together.

"*This ignorant muthafucka*" I thought.

"The term is transgender, and you ain't hitting shit!" I barked. "Hell you a Dr, you suppose to know that!"

At this point I was livid. Not only was this fool trying to get his little dirty rocks off, he had the nerve to crack on my hands being big. I tried my best to keep my composure seeing as I needed him to help put my plan in motion. All the while I was thinking "*I wonder how he would like these big ass hands wrapped around his muthafuckin throat?*" I gritted my teeth as I visualized choking the shit out of his funny looking ass, but quickly came to my senses. "*Calm down girl, remember you are a lady,*" I said to myself.

"No need to get salty with me. I suggest you check that attitude at the door the next time, unless of course you can find someone else to pull this shit off." Dr. Johnson glared at me. "If you play your cards right we both can get what we want. I like to switch teams every now and then and you will do just fine. I know you are a woman now but you still just enough man for me. Just know that this conversation doesn't leave this room. And if you even think about breathing a word of this to anyone I will expose your ass so fast you won't know what hit you. Bottom line is, if you decide to get diarrhea of the mouth just know that I will spread the word on you also."

With that he stood up and extended his hand towards me. "So do we have a deal?"

I had a huge knot in the pit of my stomach as I reluctantly shook his hand. I hated the idea of having to cheat on Adrian but I had to do whatever it took to get the job done.

"Deal"

All For Love

"Sweetheart what is it?" Adrian asked as he walked into the bedroom to see me quietly crying.

I immediately dried my eyes and tried to straighten up my appearance. I knew that I would have to tell Adrian sooner or later that I couldn't have kids and this was just as good a time as any. However, I needed to look convincing. I needed for him to believe me without a shadow of doubt so that there would be no issues with us moving forward with the surrogate.

Not only would I need to convince him that I was unable to conceive. I also needed him to use the Dr. I had chosen. Everything was all set with Dr. Johnson, well aside from the fact that the bastard wanted a little side action on top of the money I was already paying him.

I knew that if I pretended as if I didn't want him to know what was wrong he would become even more concerned with prying it out of me. Adrian was a good man and he hated seeing his baby upset.

"I'm ok," I replied softly.

"Bae I can clearly see that you are upset, you know you can talk to me. You have been acting so distant these past few weeks. I know something is bothering you."

Here goes nothing; Halle Berry didn't have shit on me, I should have won an Academy Award that day for the performance I put on.

"Sigh…. sit down Adrian. I have something that I need to tell you."

At this point he was growing increasingly concerned. The last time Pebbles said they "needed to talk" he found out that her parent weren't really dead. He had a sinking feeling that this might have something to do with her family.

"What is it bae?" he asked after taking a seat next to me on the bed.

"I went to the doctor the other day and…." I began choking up before I could get the words out.

"What is it! Are you ok? What's wrong baby?"

"I don't want you to panic, I'm fine. It's just that he confirmed what I had been suspecting for a while. Adrian I can't have children."

With that I broke down sobbing, peeping at him every now and then to see his reaction.

"Oh my God baby I'm sorry. Are you sure? We need to get a second opinion."

Adrian was visibly upset but he tried his best not to show it.

"I've already had a second and a third opinion. I wanted to be sure before I sprang it on you."

"Sprang it on me? Sweetheart this is your body we are talking about. I can't imagine you going through all of this alone, why wouldn't you tell me what's going on so I could be there for you?"

"Because I was afraid if you knew that I might not be able to have kids that you wouldn't want me anymore. I know how important a big family is to you. I just didn't want to disappoint you."

"Pebbles look at me," Adrian said softly as he turned my face towards his.

"Listen to me carefully, I'm not going anywhere, we are in this together. Yeah I want a family but you are my wife and what's important right now is your health. The only thing that I'm disappointed about is that you kept this from me. I would have been at every Dr.'s appointment right by your side. Hell for all we know it could be me and not you.

I couldn't love this man more than I did at this very moment. I should have known that he would be in my corner. Many women can only dream about having the type of man my boo was. Now that I had told him about my infertility half the battle was already won. At this point I was certain that he would have no problem with the idea of a surrogate. The next thing that needed to happen was a visit to Dr. Johnson's office. And that son of a bitch better not had breathed a word of our agreement to anyone.

"I knew it wasn't you Adrian. I always had a feeling something wasn't quite right with my body. Ever since I was a young girl I always had horrible cramps and my periods were always irregular. That's why you hardly hear me say that "I'm on." Well my suspicions were confirmed when I found out that I had scarring on my ovaries and uterus due to Endometriosis. Dr Johnson said that laparoscopy can be used to remove any scar tissue and that I could possibly conceive after that. However, the surgery is not full proof. Depending on the amount of scarring it may not be helpful at all. I could still possibly need traditional surgery which could in turn lead to more scarring. I have to be perfectly honest with you Adrian. I've been through so much with my body already, I don't know if I could take another disappointment. Not to mention the cost. If it doesn't work we would still have to explore other options."

I went on to explain to him how Dr Johnson suggested using a gestational surrogate if we still wanted to produce our own offspring instead of adoption. I explained that another woman would undergo the embryo transfer process, and then carry the pregnancy to term instead of me. This was really another key piece in the puzzle that I needed him to agree to. I hadn't been able to sleep for weeks worrying about how he would receive this information, but seeing how supportive my baby was I'm sure he won't have a problem agreeing with anything that makes me happy.

Adrian listened intently before chiming in. "Damn I had no idea you had been through so much baby. We will get through this one day at a time. One thing I don't want you to worry about is the cost. We will pay whatever it takes to get you the care you need. I love you and nothing will ever change that Pebbles. And if a surrogate is the answer then so be it. "

With that he embraced me as I wept.

"What did I do to deserve a man as good as you? I'm so lucky to have you" I whispered though the tears before planting kisses all over Adrian's face.

"I ask myself the same thing, I'm a lucky man.

Moving Forward

The visits to Dr. Johnson's office went off without a hitch. Adrian was a little hesitant at first seeing as his office wasn't in the nicest of neighborhoods. However, it didn't take much for me to convince him that I trusted this Dr. and that he treated me well. And the fact that he was highly recommend for doing artificial inseminations even though I hid the fact that his credentials were a bit sketchy.

Despite the fact that it took his ghetto ass six times to past the board he had a pretty good reputation amongst the regulars. He even took extra measures to put his game face on whenever I showed up with Adrian. He was totally professional, so much so that Adrian felt completely secure in the decision to use him as my primary care physician.

The only few times the doc showed his ass was the first time we visited his office together. The bastard had the nerve to hit me on my ass on the sly tip as we were walking out of his office. On another occasion he whispered in my ear on the way out about how rough my hands were looking that day. What the hell was it with this dude and my damn hands? Surprisingly he had yet to set a date for when were to start meeting up for me to pay of my debt. It killed me to think about cheating on Adrian because he was such a good man and he damn near worshipped the ground I walked on, but I had to do whatever it took to pull this scheme off. My man wanted a baby and I needed to pull out all the stops to get him one.

Once again the angels must have been looking out for us because we were able to hire someone rather quickly to carry the child. This woman would be carrying the love child of Adrian and I so she needed to be in tip top shape. Falynn Roberts was the surrogate that was chosen. She was a 24-year-old nursing student from a decent family. We had all the background and drug tests ran on her as well as her medical history. She was young, healthy and seemed genuinely eager to help us out. Not to mention the fact that the $50,000 check she would be receiving would be a nice nest egg for her to tuck away.

There was a clause also in the agreement that stated she would come and live with us during her final trimester; sooner if she wished. That way we could keep an eye on her and ensure that our baby was getting the best care possible. As well as be there for the delivery. Everything was right on track. I must say, I'm a bad bitch when it comes to my shit. Who else could pull something like this off and get away with it? Pretty soon my husband would have his baby and we would be one big happy family.

Dr. Strange Love

The final piece of the puzzle was the choosing my egg donor. I did this on a day when Adrian wasn't present. He actually thought I was going in to have some of my eggs extracted to be frozen. It was a bit rough convincing him that he didn't need to be present when I had the procedure done. You see ladies, that's what happens when you land a man that cares about every aspect of your wellbeing; Adrian wanted to be with me every step of the way and it took nothing short of a miracle to talk him into going into work.

It was a beautiful sunny day and I couldn't have been more excited to see what Dr. Johnson had to offer as far as donors. He already knew what I was looking for in terms of appearance and promised me that he could deliver.

"Nice to see you again Pebbles."

The Dr. greeted me as I stepped into his office.

"Thanks Dr." I replied as I sat down. As far as I was concerned he could cut all the damn formalities and get to the business at hand.

"You are looking mighty good today Pebbles" he grinned slyly as he took a seat across from me at his desk.

"Thanks doc., I really don't have time for small talk. I want to get down to business. I hope you have some fine chicks for me to choose from."

He chuckled as he spun around in his chair and grabbed the stack of photo albums that was on the table behind him.

"You know Pebbles most people care about the health of their child and worry about things like the donor's health and whether or not they have a history of mental illness, disease… things of that nature, more so than just looks. I mean these girls have been screened but still, I know looks can't be the ONLY thing you are concerned about."

"Look doc, I couldn't give a damn about that right now. I mean of course I want a healthy baby but my main concern right now is that Adrian is convinced without a shadow of a doubt that this child belongs to us. Like I said before as long as she looks good and resembles me it's all good."

I gave him the side eye for trying to overstep his damn boundaries. All I needed him to do was shut the hell up and do as he was told. Shit I wasn't paying him to be fucking Dr Oz.

"Damn she is ignorant as hell," Dr. Johnson mumbled under his breath.

"No more ignorant than your ghetto ass, now hand me a damn book!" I barked as I snatched the book out of his hands and proceeded to flip thought it.

"Aww hell naw! These bitches are all wrong," I exclaimed.

"This one looks like she got a lazy eye; this one here got a damn bell pepper nose, and what's up with all these hoes with no neck? This bitch looks like Nelly! Oh no, you gotta come better than this doc. And are these recent pictures? I hope it ain't no damn photo shop and Instagram filters on here. How do they booty look? I want my baby to be stacked like me."

"Stacked like you? Your shit is fake…, and how do you even know it's going to be a girl?" Dr. Johnson asked with a look of disgust on his face. "You know what, never mind…."

Dr. Johnson was trying to act all brand new; like he was better than me just because I had standards on how I wanted my child to look. Hell truth be told I had been mistaken for Beyoncé several times since my sex change. That's probably why this bastard was admiring my fine ass.

It was true; despite the fact that Pebbles was ignorant, ghetto, and as messy as they came the doc couldn't deny the fact that her ratchet ass disposition was turning him on.

"I like this one right here doc. She's cute and looks like me and Beyoncé. I REALLY do kinda look like Beyoncé," I said as I admired myself in the mirror in his office. "I can see how people would mistake me for her."

I glanced over to see the doc damn near foaming at the mouth. "You might look like Beyoncé but them hands lookin like Jay Z."

What the fuck? That's it I ain't taking no more cracks on my damn hands! The nerve! A lady can only take so much before she has to show her true colors. It was time I put the Dr. in his place.

"Let me tell you something doc. All the money in the world don't give you the right to keep breakin' on my hands. They may look manly in your opinion but my boo likes them. I suggest you watch your damn mouth before one of these *manly hands* slaps your ass into next week.

"I would love nothing more," he replied looking at me downright sinister.

"What the hell are you talking about you ole pervert?"

"You heard me right. I would love nothing more than for you to slap me around with those bear claws of yours. I've been watching those big ass knuckles ever since you walked in here and I just want you to know it's all good! Just watching you turn them pages done got me hard as hell."

With that Dr. Johnson pushed away from his desk with his rolling chair to reveal his four inch micro peen on rock hard. Not only had this fucker exposed himself and was jacking off under the desk, to make matters worse he was getting off on my damn hands!

"Ugh! What the hell? Put that little shit away! Da fuck wrong with you? Your ass about to make me forget I'm a lady and a Christian." I recoiled in disgust. I mean who does shit like this? I know I'm fine and all but damn! I didn't know I was running niggas crazy like this? Lawd and look at how small that shit is. Hell my reconstructed clit was bigger than this nub.

"Ha haaaa, call me what you like but you putting them paws on me today," he panted as he continued to stoke himself with his index finger and his thumb. "Put them man hands on me Pebbles, please."

I was livid. No this asshole didn't want me to jack him off.

"I'm not touching your shriveled up ass dick. You are a sick man doc."

"Sick for you baby. Come on nigga put them hands on me like the man I know you are underneath all that shit."

That was the straw that broke the camel's back! I walked over to the doctor and hit his ass so damn hard I knocked his wiglet cockeyed on his head. Before I knew it this fool was getting off, thrashing around in his seat as I slapped his ass repeatly. The more I cussed and abuse him the harder he came. The doc had some kind of sick man hand fetish.

Not to mention the fact that he loved the abuse I was dishing out. By the time the whole ordeal was over I thought I would vomit.

"Thank you so much Pebbles, you don't know how long I had been fantasizing about that" he bellowed as he stood up and straightened his wiglet.

"Glad I could be of service," I responded sarcastically. "I tell you what; put me down for this young lady right here and let's call it a day. I'm outta here."

With that I grabbed my purse and headed out of his office.

"Call me mittens!" he chirped as I slammed the door behind me.

On the ride home I had to pull over to a 7/11 and grab a small pack of soda crackers to settle my stomach before I made it home. Adrian and I were going out to dinner tonight and this fool had not only taken my appetite; he had completely turned my stomach.

Here I was thinking all this damn time he wanted some ass from me and all he keeps talking about is my damn hands. I mean at the end of the day I'm glad I didn't have to cheat on Adrian by fucking his ass; and Lawd knows ain't shit attractive about his old ass but damn, I never saw this shit coming. I hope I can hold out for as long as I need him. There was nothing I could do but keep these hands ashy and hope for the best, I glanced over at them on the steering wheel as I drove home.

"Sigh… I really do need to give Dr. Yoon a call."

Once the baby was born I might have to pay him a visit.

Stay In Ya Lane

6 months later

My life had been a whirlwind. Adrian and I finally moved into our new place; a gorgeous four bedroom raised ranch in an affluent African American sub division. My job was going better than even and my baby had even gotten himself a promotion at the Athletic Physical Therapy hospital he started at once we got married. And last but not least we were about to become parents. Even though I wasn't carrying the child it was an indescribable feeling of joy and happiness sharing this bond with my husband. Just knowing that I was able to give him one of the things that he wanted the most in this world; a child gave me a deep sense of satisfaction.

Yes I had been able to pull everything off without a hitch. I was bad bitch to say the least. I mean how many women do you know would go the extents that I have to keep my man happy? These little birds out here in the game now could stand to learn a thing or two from me. I mean less face it; I was cut from a different mold. I can't help it that I'm that chick. I didn't choose the diva life, the diva life chose me.

Hell it's a good thing I got married when I did. Ain't no telling how many hearts I would be breaking if I were still single. I can see it now I would be every man's pet and every woman's threat. Yeah that right I said it. I'm that chick bitches WISH they could be. The only thorns in my side at this point were the damn freaky ass Dr. with his crazy ass hand fetish and the surrogate, Falynn.

Dr. Johnson had resorted to buying all kinds of damn lace and fingerless gloves and shit for me to wear when I made visits to his office. The scenario was always the same. Either he would jack off while rubbing and kissing on my hands or the fucker would want me to rub all over his big ass beer belly while he whacked away. Very rarely did he want me to touch that eraser dick of his because it would always result in him getting off no sooner than I touched it, which was fine with me.

I guess I really can't complain considering the fact that at least I didn't have to fuck the bastard. Problem is now he was obsessed. Every time I looked up his ass was calling talking about my damn hands! Well I got a trick for him. Once the baby gets a few months old I'm paying a plastic surgeon a visit. I had already spoken to someone and he assured me that could he make my hands appear smaller by shaving down my knuckles a bit. He also suggested that I have laser resurfacing done on them to soften them up a bit more. I planned on making an appointment for this as soon as possible. This freak would no longer be able to get his thrills off on my damn hands. Besides it pissed me off that he found the only thing that was still remotely masculine about me to get off on. Sigh… what's a girl to do?

As far as Falynn was concerned, I guess she was nice enough. She had just moved into one of the spare bedrooms. We had turned one into an office and the other into a nursery for the baby. I tried my best to be civil but at the end of the day I had to admit to myself that I felt some kind of way about her living here. I mean I know she's carrying our baby and all but I don't like the idea of another bitch all up in the house with my man; a young pretty bitch at that. It was all good though. As long as she knew her place and stayed out of my way and out of my man's face we wouldn't have any problems. I only had three more months to play along then I could send her ass packin'.

Current day

"Hey bae" Adrian announced as he walked through the door and planted a kiss on my lips.

"Wassup boo? How was your day?"

"It was good; they worked the hell out of me today."

I was just about to ask him if he wanted a massage before dinner when he shot past me and headed to the family room where Falynn was watching TV.

"How's my little one doing?" he asked as he bent down on one knee to rub her belly.

"No this nigga didn't," I thought to myself.

"We're doing well, I ate some hot wings at lunch time, and they had him kicking like crazy," Falynn giggled.

Adrian laughed as he took a seat. He and Falynn made small talk, chatting it up about the baby. You would think the nigga would at least take his work clothes off and get comfortable first. This was becoming an annoying ass habit. Every day he would damn near knock my ass over to get next to this bitch. And what's up with all this damn belly rubbing? I was definitely gonna have a talk with his ass after dinner.

When Adrian finally decided get up and leave the room Falynn stopped him on the way out.

"Hang on a minute he's kicking right now," she announced, beckoning Adrian back in.

He looked like a damn kid in a candy store each time he felt his son moving. There was no denying the fact that he loved this child although it wasn't here yet. He had tears in his eyes each time he heard the heartbeat. Somehow I felt like this child was also filling a void that he was experiencing from the loss of his sister.

"Bae! Come here quick!" he yelled.

I could feel my blood boiling as I walked in to see him caressing Falynn's pregnant belly. I'm not gonna lie I was a bit envious of this bitch. I wanted that to be me getting this attention from my husband. And quiet as it was kept it did hurt me that I wasn't the one carrying his child. I had successfully transformed my body to look like a woman but that was the one thing that money couldn't buy; a uterus. Ahhh well you win some, you lose some.

I played the shit off and walked over to her. Falynn gently took my hand and placed it on her warm round belly. This was the first time I had actually felt a pregnant woman's stomach and I must admit the experience was pretty amazing, all the negative feelings that I was having just a few minutes prior went by the wayside when I felt our son moving.

"I felt it!" I exclaimed.

AJ was in there kicking away! This was a tender family moment between me and my baby. It was as though Falynn wasn't even in the room even though she was the one with the child in her belly.

Adrian looked at me and kissed me on the forehead.

"I can't wait till our son gets here" he whispered.

"Neither can I, you're going to make a good daddy."

"Thanks bae."

I was snapped back into reality by Falynn placing Adrian's hand on her right side where AJ could now be felt kicking. I know she had just done the same thing with me but I didn't like her touching my man. This was just as bad if not worse than him running in to feel all on her big ass belly every day.

"Bitch he can figure out where the baby is moving. He don't need no damn assistance!" I thought.

That was it. I'm having a few words with his ass today for sure!

Her Or Me

I couldn't wait for dinner to end and I finally had Adrian all to myself. While he was in our room relaxing I popped in.

"I need to talk to you."

"About what?"

Adrian could tell by the look on my face and the tone in my voice that I was clearly upset about something, he just didn't know what. His look also read that he really didn't want to hear the shit right now but he obliged me anyway.

"I want to talk about how you are always up in Falynn's face."

"What the hell you talking about Pebbles?" he asked as he looked over at me frowning.

"I'm talking about how you be sprinting like you in the damn Olympics to get to her every day when you walk in the door. Your ass be running to her like you Usian Bolt and shit.

Hell you barely acknowledge me before you running to find her and speak. I don't even get a chance to hardly ask you about your day before you rushing to rub her damn belly! And I won't even go there with the fact that half the damn time you don't even ask me how my day was."

I was fuming. I stood with my arms folded as I waited on his response.

Before I knew it he had stood to his feet.

"I can't believe you going there with this bullshit Pebbles. You know how excited I am about this baby? Hell ain't nobody thinking about that girl."

"I can't tell, the way you fawn all over her like she's the damn second coming."

"Ok let's get one thing straight," Adrian responded. By now he was mad his damn self. He couldn't believe that he was being accused of giving this chick more attention than his wife.

"I don't like the way you came up in here and fronted on me. This shit right here is petty. Hell if you don't know I love you by now you will never know. "And let me ask you this? What exactly are you accusing me of? Are you trying to say I'm pushing up on the damn surrogate?"

Adrian was hot. I had pissed him off in the past with my insecurities but this really seemed to send him over the edge. I knew that he loved me and I also knew that he wouldn't hurt me by betraying my trust. I just couldn't help my jealousy.

"You didn't hear me say that."

"You might as well have said it. The way you busted up in here to check me. I don't want any other woman besides you but I can't keep catering to your damn insecurities. That's something you are going to have to deal with on your own. I'm done with it."

With that Adrian waved his hand, turned the TV back up and laid back down.

"No this asshole is not going to just dismiss my feelings that easy," I thought. *"I see I have to take another route with his ass."*

It was true I should have approached him differently and I might have gotten different response. I mean the way I came on him what could I expect?

"Adrian would you at least hear me out?" I asked as I walked over and manually turned the TV back down causing him to roll his eyes at me.

I sat down on the bed with him and softened my tone.

"I'm sorry I ran in here on you like that. I know you love me and I trust you. I'm embarrassed to admit this, but it's just that ever since I found out that I can't have kids I feel like less of a woman."

Adrian turned the TV off and gave me his undivided attention.

"I know you consider my insecurities petty but it goes deeper than that for me. I already had issues with the way I came up and all. And now this; I finally get to be with the man I love and I can't even give him a child. Someone else has to carry it. It just gets to me sometimes that's all. And when I see you walk in the door and rush to her yes it makes me angry and jealous, not because I feel like you want her over me. I'm just envious over the fact that I want to be the one carrying your child. I wanted to be the one to give you that gift but I can't.

You just don't know how it feels to want something so badly but to know that it will never happen. I want to be the one sharing that experience with you. I want you taking pictures of my belly as it grows, videotaping the delivery, the whole nine yards, but I have to live with the fact every day that it will never happen."

Adrian reached over and wiped the tear that was about to fall on my cheek before giving me a tight hug.

"Baby I'm so sorry. That never even crossed my mind."

"It's ok; I know I'm a mess all the way around," I whimpered.

Adrian released his embrace and looked at me.

"No you are not. You are remarkable a woman that's been through a lot of pain and I should be more sensitive to it. I'm sorry for making light about your feelings. I can't even imagine what is must be like for you. I'm just so excited knowing our baby is on the way. The attention you see me giving Falynn is only because I want to make sure she is well taken care of and nothing more. I want her to be comfortable and deliver us a healthy child and that's as far as it goes."

"I know…"

"Listen Pebbles nothing or nobody is worth driving a wedge in my marriage. I love you and if that means me pulling back a bit with Falynn then so be it. From now on you will be the only woman I run to when I walk in the door."

"You would do that for me?"

"Damn right! I can't have my baby unhappy. You are so beautiful Pebbles. I hope he has your eyes."

I batted my lashes at him and gave him a peck on the lips.

That was it. Just as quickly as we fought we had made up.

The next few weeks were much easier on me. Adrian had pulled back the attention that he was giving Falynn drastically. He still asked her how she was doing every day and even gave the occasional belly rub but it was nothing like it had been before. I was back on top! As long as my husband knew his place with two women in the house everything would be fine from here on out. He just needed a little reminding of who the head bitch in charge was, and as long as Falynn stayed in her lane it was blue skies ahead.

The Rise Of Falynn

"I know that muthafucka must have said something to him," Falynn said to herself as she rubbed her firm round belly.

"He has barely paid me any attention these past few weeks."

She looked around the beautifully decorated bedroom and began speaking to the unborn child.

"I really do love living here. I could see myself staying forever. Adrian is such a good man and he needs a good woman. Hell I'm the one carrying his child. I think the three of us would make a beautiful family. Don't worry baby, momma is gonna make sure you are well taken care of. I just need to set some things straight. It's about time I read that bitch Pebbles."

Little to Pebbles and Adrian's knowledge Falynn had plans of her own. She too was playing a role. She came off as the sweet innocent surrogate but in reality she had an entirely different agenda that was soon to be revealed. It was imperative that she played her part in front of Adrian seeing as she had made up her mind that she wanted him for herself. However this would not be the case in front of Pebbles. She would wait till her day off so that the two of them would be home alone together then she would make her move. She had every intention of letting Pebbles know that she knew that she was the reason why Adrian was so stand offish and she didn't like it one bit.

When the day finally came Falynn made sure she was up early and sitting in the kitchen when Pebbles walked in. Normally she would chill in her bedroom most of the day till it was time for Adrian to get off work then she would purposely make her way to the family room. However this wasn't the case today. Falynn poured herself a glass of orange juice and propped herself up on one of the high pub chairs in front of the winding countertop and waited. When Pebbles walked in she was a bit surprised to see her out and about so early.

"Oh hey, good morning," I greeted Falynn as I poured myself a cup of coffee.

"So, what did you say to him?" Falynn asked sarcastically.

"*Damn this bitch can't even say good morning?*" I thought "Say to who?" I asked looking confused.

"Adrian, I know you said something to him. That's why he hasn't been paying me any attention lately."

"*What the hell was this trick talking about?*" I thought to myself. "*I KNOW this hoe ain't questioning what I say to my man.*"

"Excuse me? You waaaay outta your lane! I know you didn't just question me on what I talk to MY man about." I had to put her ass in check with the quickness!

"Nigga please!" Falynn responded just as sharply as she had been addressed.

"What's the matter, cat got ya tounge? You heard me right, NIGGA PLEASE."

Falynn repeated her response. "You standing there looking all shocked and shit. I wanna know what you said to Adrian. He hasn't said two words to me since your jealous ass confronted him about rubbing my belly."

I could feel my damn blood pressure rising. Who in the fuck did this bitch think she was talking to? I had a feeling this heffa wanted my man and this shit right here just confirmed it.

"You got me all fucked up if you think you gon' run your narrow ass up in here and steal my man. I knew it was something about your ass; I just couldn't put my finger on it. You might have Adrian fooled but I got your damn number. You better be glad you carrying that damn baby or…"

"Or what? Boy bye!" Falynn waived her hand and spun the chair around to turn her back to me.

"What the hell is this bitch talkin about?" I thought. I wanted to know what was with all this referencing me as a man. I gave myself a quick once over in the mirror that was in the

hallway. Shit, just as I thought. I knew I looked good. Somebody must have put this bitch on to me and I intended to find out who it was. That damn Dr. Johnson had better not been running his mouth. I walked over to that hoe and looked her dead in her damn eyes.

"What the hell you talking about Falynn; you trying to be a funny bitch saying that I look like a man?"

"I ain't TRYING to say shit. You heard me right the first time bro. Now I suggest you get the fuck out of my face!"

"You keep referring to me as a man but that jaw of yours is looking kinda strong while you trying to talk about somebody."

Falynn laughed "ok dude, if that's what makes you feel better."

With that she got out of her seat and thought she was going to walk away from me but I wasn't having it. This bitch was not only trying to check me about my man but she was trying to be funny and shit, sneering and making man comments. If she thought it was going to end there she had another thing coming. I was getting to the bottom of this shit today!

"Look Falynn I done been more than patient with your trifling ass. If you got something on your mind I suggest you spill it. You got something you wanna say to me? What is it jealously? That's what it is isn't it? I can see it in your eyes. You want to be in my shoes don't you bitch?"

"*This nigga right here is TRULY delusional,*" Falynn thought to herself, smirking as she listened to Pebbles pompous ass rant.

"Listen Falynn, I know your ass done got all comfy and shit laying up in my damn house but make no mistake, this is MY house. I make the rules. I know Adrian and I have the perfect relationship that any woman would be envious of but the bottom line is you gotta get your own man, he is off limits.

I mean I don't blame you for wanting my life, who wouldn't? Hell if you had played your cards right I might have even given your sorry ass a few tips on how to step ya game up, but you done fucked that all up by not staying in ya lane. So I suggest you have your ass a seat." I smiled as I fluffed my hair and pouted my lips at that hoe. I couldn't wait for this bitch to be out of my house. Not only did she want my man, the bitch wanted to be me!

Falynn couldn't believe what she was hearing. *"The audacity of this manly muthafucka thinking I was jealous of HIS ass!"* she thought. It was at that point that she had listened to all she could take. Pebbles was truly a fucking nutcase and it was time somebody knocked her ass down a few notches.

Falynn was about to go in her room when she quickly turned around to stand toe to toe with me following close on her heels.

"I knew your ass was crazy but I didn't know you were delusional also. Answer me this; why would I want to be in your shoes?

With yo' big ass feet! Why the hell would I want the life of a murderer?" Falynn raised her eyebrow and waited for my response.

I stood there in silence, shock and disbelief. How in the hell did she know I had killed someone? At that very moment I felt as if my whole world was about to come crashing in. The scene of me slicing Tasha's throat flashed before my eyes. I had tried my damndest to put that whole experience behind me. It was bad enough that Adrian was constantly talking about her and now here this bitch stood as a blatant reminder. I wanted to snap that bitch's neck on the spot but she was carrying our child. Besides if she knew others could know as well. I had to pull back and dig a bit more. I had to find out exactly what she knew.

"Murderer? What the hell you talking about?" I tried my best to play it cool but the look on my face said otherwise.

Falynn busted out laughing. "You should see the look on your damn face. What's the matter Peyton? Tasha's ghost done came back to haunt your crazy ass?"

"Peyton? Tasha?" I had started sweating and my heart was racing a mile a minute. I had been exposed! I tried my best to look confused as though I didn't know what she was talking about but it wasn't working, this bitch had my number.

Falynn went in her room and sat on the bed.

"I'm a little tired today so I'm gonna stop toying with your simple ass." She was perfectly relaxed as she stretched out on the bed.

"You mighty damn brave to be laying your ass down in front of me after all that shit you just talked," I snapped.

Even though she was on to me she TRULY had no idea who she was dealing with. I would snuff this bitch's lights out in a heartbeat and start again from scratch before I let her fuck up all of my hard work! My eyes were narrow as slits as I gave her a vexing stare that would cut through ice. "You might be carrying that baby in your belly but that won't stop me from knocking you upside your mutha fuckin' head" I barked as I stood over her, picturing myself tossing her ass straight into the damn amour.

Falynn propped herself up with the plush throw pillows that were on her bed and leaned against the headboard.

"You wouldn't do that because you want this baby too bad. Or should I say you NEED this baby. Have a seat Peyton while I lay out my list of demands."

"List of demands?"

I couldn't believe it! This hoe was going to try and blackmail me! Falynn had proven herself a worthy opponent. I had no choice but to humble myself and see what this bitch had to say.

After taking a seat in the rocking chair that sat in the corner of her room, I watched as Falynn opened her nightstand drawer and pulled out a journal.

"First things first, I saw you kill your friend that morning. You thought no one saw you but I did."

My mouth dropped open. I was utterly speechless. I thought I had covered all my tracks! How in the hell did she see me? It was dark outside plus I was wearing a mask. There was no way, it just wasn't possible. This heffa must be bluffing. I didn't say a word. Instead I let her continue on.

"I was staying with my grandparents at the time. They just happened to live on the same street as your friend Tasha. I was mad because I had gotten into an argument with my parents the night before. My grandma started in on me extra early that morning about how I needed to start taking responsibility for my actions and how I needed to stop giving my parents so much grief. Bottom line is I didn't want to hear the shit. I stormed out of the house and sat in the car.

I turned it on for a little while to warm it up but my grandmother started talking shit out the doorway about wasting her gas so I killed the engine. After she went back in the house I sat in the car and pouted for the next half hour. That's when I noticed someone dressed in all black slip beside the house across the street. I slid down in my seat so I wouldn't be seen and waited to see what was about to happen. Little did I know I was about to witness a damn murder."

"When the lady in the house came out someone grabbed her from behind. I couldn't see exactly what was going on. All I know is whoever it was left her ass lying in the driveway in a pool of blood with the car running."

"Now seeing as I'm a bitch that's on her grind that desperately needed to hit a lick so I could move the hell away from my grandparent's house, I decided to follow the person who killed Tasha."

I sat back in disbelief as Falynn shared her story of how she followed me to my house and cased me out for days till she finally got a good look at me in the daytime.

"Yo' crazy ass wasn't scared to follow me after you saw me kill somebody?" I knew this was an admission of guilt but hell I had already been found out. This bitch seemed to be 'bout that life and I needed to see just how far she was planning to take this little witch hunt of hers.

"Hell naw! I ain't scared of shit, plus I was packin heat my damn self. Don't let the pretty face fool you. Anyway I figured whoever killed this chick must have a reason to want her dead. And They THOUGHT the dirty deed went unseen, but I saw that shit with my own two eyes. I just needed to find out who was behind the mask and what the motive was. That's when I started casing your ass every day.

With that Falynn handed me a manila folder. Inside were pictures of me entering my house through the side door the morning of the murder. This bitch had pictures of me dressed in the all black as well as shots of me coming and going in my everyday attire. She had my home address in the shots, license plate number and everything. How in the hell could I have slipped like this?

"How did you get these?" I asked as I frantically flipped through the photos.

"I know you can't be that dumb" she laughed as she picked up her Iphone and waved it at me. "I never leave home without it. A hustler stays prepared for anything. A bitch like me never knows when she's gon' run up on some shit she needs proof of later on."

"Is this all you have? These pictures don't prove shit." I said calmly as a million thoughts were running through my head. I couldn't let this skank have the upper hand on me. No matter what, I couldn't show fear. I had to stay the course till I figured out how to dispose of her ass once and for all.

Falynn laughed, "Oh I have way more than just pictures. After I followed your ass and gathered some information I passed it on to one of my niggas who works as a private investigator."

"Hoe this ain't no damn CSI, you know damn well you ain't got no damn money for a private investigator. Who the hell do you think you bullshittin'?" I stared that bitch down to let her know that I wasn't about to be moved by her fake ass story. She was fronting like she had so much on my ass when in reality all she had was some damn pictures that could easily be destroyed.

"Oh contraire Peyton, haven't you heard the song? Never trust a big butt and a smile? Having your sorry ass checked out was as easy as letting my boy sample some of this good ass pussy of mine. Funny thing is; you weren't even worth the fuck. He gave me all the information I needed on your ass just for letting him taste it."

"Besides the murder I know about your ass going overseas to have a sex change, your hoeing and stripping, AND how your sorry ass is playing Adrian. This is really some lowdown shit you doing. Damn dude, I be hearing you on the phone. You didn't even tell your parents? Hell even I wouldn't go that far!"

"Get thee behind me Satan!" I screamed. "Lawd I done let the devil up in here! You can't judge me! Only God can judge me! I did what I had to for love. That's something you young ass tricks wouldn't know nothing about!" At this point I had jumped out of my seat and started pacing the room before finally catching myself. I was letting this bitch see me sweat and it wasn't a good look.

"Love? You murdered your best friend Peyton, for a damn man!" Falynn shook her head at what she was hearing.

"The devil is a lie! My name is Pebbles!" I yelled.

I looked over to see Falynn bent over in laughter about to fall off the bed. "Stop it please, my bladder is weak. You gon' make me piss on myself."

"Oh you think the shit is funny!" I raged. Before I knew it my temper had gotten the best of me. I raked everything on Falynn's dresser onto the floor and put my fist through the 32 inch T.V. screen.

"You betta calm your crazy ass down!" Falynn yelled as she jumped to her feet."

"Or what bitch? Huh? I finally got a rise out of your silly ass didn't I? One thing you betta get through your thick ass skull real quick is I don't have a problem fucking you up. You saw what I did to my friend so what makes you think I would spare your ass any pain and suffering if you try and get in my way?" I replied as I ran up on that bitch with every intention of dotting her damn eye! Fuck the plan, this bitch had crossed the line and it was about to be some furniture moved today!

Despite the fact that Falynn was talking a good game she had to admit to herself this muthafucka was on some other shit at this point. Pebbles' fury had frightened her to the point she felt like she needed to protect herself.

When Pebbles ran up on her she quickly went in her pocket and pulled out her mace and sprayed her directly in the face.

"Ahhhh!!!" I shrieked in pain as the liquid hit my face like a flamethrower. This bitch had maced me! I wanted to kill her ass but all I could do was roll around on the floor screaming and covering my eyes. "When I get straight Imma kill yo' ass bitch! You betta' run while you got the chance!"

"Look Peyton!"

"The name is Pebbles!"

"Bow down bitch, I been on. I been a woman all my life. You just getting on and done lost your damn mind. I didn't want to do it. I told you to calm your ass down. Now you can act like you got some damn sense or I can let your ass have it again. What's it gon' be?"

Falynn stood over me with a bold authoritative tone to her voice. She was in complete control. She placed her foot on my neck as I writhed around on the floor in pain. I was defeated. When it was all said and done I had no choice but to crawl my sorry ass to the bathroom and douse my face with cold water. When the burning finally subsided I looked in the mirror and saw that my face was red and swollen and my eyes were bloodshot. That bitch had pulled a fast one on me.

"How the hell you gon' mace me Falynn? That shit just ain't right. You didn't have to do me like that."

"You tried to run up and got a surprise. Just like the one you gon' get if you even THINK about retaliating. Keep that in mind if you try to creep your crazy ass in here tonight. I will have something under the pillow waiting for your ass. Now back to the business at hand. I need to lay out my demands and YOU have to clean this damn mess up before Adrian gets home. I don't know how you gon' explain that TV."

I looked over at the mess I had made, and for what? I was at Falynn's mercy and I had no choice but to oblige her wishes, at least for the moment. *I gotta get this shit cleaned up and hit Best Buy real quick to grab another TV and get rid of the old one before Adrian gets home this evening*," I thought.

I walked back over to the rocking chair where I had originally been seated, took a seat and patted my face and eyes with the cool damp rag.

"Tell me what you want."

"That's more like it," Falynn declared as she rubbed her palms together. "I knew you would eventually come around to seeing things my way. Especially considering you don't have a leg to stand on.

The first thing I want to discuss is money. I will be needed an additional $100,000 on top of the fee that we agreed upon. However, this will be our little secret. As far as Adrian knows I'm only getting $50,000 as planned for carrying the child."

"You sound like a damn fool!" I hissed. I was seething. There was no way I was going to let this bitch muscle this kind of money out of me.

Falynn frowned and raised her voice. "You ain't in no position to be turning down shit. I make the rules from here on out" she barked.

The look on her face and the base in her voice made her message come across loud and clear. There was one thing for certain; this bitch was not going to be moved. I decided that I may as well let this hoe get everything off her chest that she needed to say. Otherwise we could be at this shit all day. And besides, my damn face and eyes were swollen and still burning. I needed to lie down for a few hours and get myself together before I started on all the other shit I needed to do that day. I would have to deal with this bitch later, but for now I had to chill.

"I understand" I said calmly.

Falynn grinned and took a sip of her juice before continuing on. She seemed quite pleased that she THOUGHT she had the upper hand on me. And truth be told, she did, for the moment at least, but make no mistake, the payback I had in store for this bitch would be epic.

"I've also decided that I want Adrian for myself seeing as I'm carrying his baby. I've grown attached to little AJ" she announced looking down at her belly and giving it a pat. "You might as well say I'm his momma since I'm carrying him. I think we would make a beautiful family. Besides I don't know how I feel about my child being raised by a man" with that she shot a menacing glance in my direction.

I couldn't help but fidget in my seat. If I wasn't afraid this trollop wouldn't mace me again I would I would put this size 12 all up in her ass.

"Oh I know you mad as hell," she laughed. "Especially after all the shit you went through to get him, leading a double life and shit. I mean damn, where they do that at? If you really and truly cared about Adrian you would bow out like a real man and let him be happy with a real woman. And let this child have a normal life.

Imma keep it 100 with you Peyton. You had a pretty good scheme going but you got messy and I slid right in on your ass. Once I drop this baby weight. I intend on making Adrian feel real good. He's been so use to that old manufactured pussy of yours that he probably forgot how a real woman gets down. Oh yeah I intend to whip it on his ass real good," she purred as she groped her breast and gyrated her hips. I've been watching his fine ass since I got here. I bet he got a big dick don't he? Never mind, you don't have to answer. I'll find out soon enough.

At this point I was having an out of body experience. The vein in my forehead was starting to protrude and my left eye was starting to twitch. I visualized myself jumping up, breaking that damn glass of juice and shoving the jagged edge straight through her damn heart. I sat in complete silence as she continued to tell me how she not only planned on taking Adrian from me and raising our child, she also wanted monthly payments of $5,000 on top of the $100,000 to stay quiet about Tasha's murder.

And to add insult to injury this heffa wanted me to cook for her as well. She must really be stuck on stupid to even entertain the thought of me touching her food after all she was putting my family through. It was all good though, I'll cook for her. As a matter of fact I'll make that bitch a meal she won't ever forget. When I get finish with this hoe she gon' wish she never darkened my doorstep.

When I finally left her room I took a double shot of Remy and smoked a blunt before putting an icepack on my swollen face and lying down for the next few hours.

Day From Hell

"Uhhm hmm I got something for Peyton's punk ass if he even thinks about trying some shit with me. I wish a nigga would run up on me. I'll have his ass running back to Korea for some more damn reconstructive surgery if he fucks with me. I'll burn his shit down to the bone," Falynn said as she pulled the locked metal box from under her bed and examined its contents.

Inside was a bottle of acid which she planned on throwing in Pebbles face if she ever caught her off guard and she needed to defend herself again. There were also several more cans of mace, a Smith and Wesson revolver, three Chinese stars, a straight razor and a police Taser. She knew the risk that she was taking by living in the house with a killer so she couldn't take any chances, especially considering the fact that she would be the one to snatch the rug right from under Pebbles feet.

Falynn had never been in a situation like this before but she had enough sense to know that the more the walls closed in on Pebbles she would become more dangerous then she already was. She knew that she had to protect herself and the unborn child at all cost, and today was stone cold proof that her instincts didn't lead her wrong. There was no telling how things could have taken a turn for the worse if she wasn't carrying mace on her at the time.

"Imma always have me something ready for that nigga," she said as she placed the taser under her pillow. "He creep up in here tonight imma fry his ass like some sizzlean."

A few hours later

"Well at least the swelling has gone down," I said to myself as I gazed upon my reflection the bedroom mirror. The realization of what had happened earlier still left me feeling like all my hard work was about to be washed down the drain. There was a major security breech and her name was Falynn. This was a brazen bitch and she must be stopped. However, there was no time to construct a plan right now. I quickly ran and grabbed the busted TV from Falynn's room and moved it to the back seat of my car. I then drove it around the block to the 7/11 dumpster and dropped it off before returning and sweeping up her room.

"You missed a spot," she sneered as she pointed at the broken glass that had found its way behind her dresser.

I never said a word. Instead I worked diligently to clean the room till it was just as I had found it.

"While you were sleep I made a list of all my shit you destroyed. Imma need everything replaced today. I had planned on wearing my Viva La Juicy so you need to stop by the mall also."

I snatched the list out of her hand and headed out the door for Best Buy. Just as I was pulling into the lot my phone rang for like the 20th time. It was the damn doctor!

"What the hell could this nigga possibly want?" I fumed. I had already told him that we couldn't have our little session today. I had too much on my plate to be putting up with his damn foolishness. He would have to rub his own stomp today.

After I made the rounds and replaced the TV and all Falynn's toiletries that I had destroyed I set everything back in its place and reconnected the cable. I finally let out a sigh of relief and wiped the sweat from my brow after finishing all my tasks.

"Good job now was it really worth it?" Falynn asked as I was leaving her room.

"Fuck you bitch" I said and slammed the door behind me.

I had just enough time to get rid of the box from the new TV, take a shower and apply fresh makeup before Adrian got home. Thank God he was running a little late. It even gave me time to whip up a quick Caesars chicken salad and pop open a bottle of white wine before he walked in.

"Hey boo," I said as I planted a kiss on his lips and took his jacket.

"Hey baby!" He exclaimed as he kicked his shoes off and plopped down at the kitchen table grinning from ear to ear.

This was totally out of character for him. Even though he had slowed up with the attention he was giving Falynn he at least always addressed her, after me of course. Something else had him excited today. I wanted to know what had him so wound up.

"What's got you so happy?" I asked.

"There's been a break in the case" he beamed as he opened up the briefcase he walked in the door with and fired up his laptop.

"In the case?"

"Bae I can't believe you are asking what case. I told you that I have been working with a detective since Tasha's murder to help find her killer."

"Oh yeah, that case" I said, desperately trying not to sound disappointed. My mind began to race "*Damn!*" I thought, "*Could my day get any worse?*" I did remember that he was working with the police but I tried my best to block it out every time he talked about it. Each time he brought up the subject of Tasha it resurfaced painful memories that I struggled every day to forget.

Hell I didn't WANT to kill her but she left me no choice. Up until now I thought I had my shit trump tight but now I wasn't so sure. This new "break" in the case could lead the police closer to me, but I just couldn't see how. I had covered all my tracks However Falynn was a painful reminder that my ass was nowhere near out of the woods. My grandmother use to always say that every shut eye ain't sleep. And Falynn's big ass eyes had seen me. And now this shit. Let me see what he's talking about before I panic.

"Sooo, what did they find out?" I asked nervously.

"Well besides going through the list of people who could have a possible motive to kill her they found a footprint. It appears to be from a man's size 10 shoe, or a 12 in women's."

"Oh Shit! There was no snow that day? How did they find a footprint?" I thought.

"A footprint? Where did they find it at?"

"Apparently there was one left in the pool of blood that Tasha was left lying in. They also found a few more leading down the alley behind her house. Those forensic guys are some bad mutha fuckas! They said they were running the print against a data base of boot manufactures. Once they found the make they would narrow down a list of retailers that sold that style and possibly names and credit card numbers of everyone in the area with that boot.

They also said whoever grabbed her from behind left fibers from their clothes on her neck. Damn bae don't you just love technology?"

Adrian was ecstatic. He couldn't have been more thrilled than if Tasha was still alive.

"Clothing fibers? Footprints? That doesn't prove anything," I responded frantically. I spoke before I thought but I couldn't help it. The pressure was becoming too much and I was starting to lose it.

"Damn Pebbles there you go again trying to bust my damn bubble! If the police feel like its good enough to be considered proof why do you have to shoot it down?"

"I'm sorry Adrian but I just feel like we should be moving forward instead of backwards. I mean we about to bring a new life into the world and here you are still living in the past. I know you love you sister but at some point you have to move forward and let it go."

"Can you hear yourself talking?" he asked as he stood from his seat. "Do you know how selfish you sound right now? Let's get something straight right now. Number one there is no timetable of when I'm supposed to get over my sister's death. If I grieve her the rest of my damn days then so been it. It's no sweat off of your back so I don't understand why it's such a huge damn deal every time her name is brought up. Number two, I made a vow to catch the son of a bitch who did this to her and you can best believe I will go to my grave keeping that promise."

Adrian was livid he stood over me and glared at me like he knew I was the killer. I had never seen him this angry. Tasha's death seemed to bring out emotions in him that he would otherwise suppress. There was no way he would give up on looking for her killer and he wanted to make damn sure I knew it. The only problem was I didn't want to hear the shit. I mean damn she was dead and there was no bringing her back. I wanted to tell his ass that very thing but he was already looking at me like I was his damn enemy. I knew I had better leave well enough alone and try and defuse the situation.

"I'm sorry bae..."

"Nah don't say shit to me Pebbles. I can't believe you went there as bad as you know I miss my sister. You done fucked up my whole vibe."

He sat back down and continued to look over his paperwork.

Just as luck would have it Falynn's nosey ass had been listening to our conversation the whole time and decided that she would pop in and stick her big ass nose where it didn't belong.

"That's great news Adrian!" she said as she stood behind him looking over his shoulder at the notes he had pulled out of his briefcase.

"Thanks Falynn, I'm glad somebody thinks so," he griped as he shuffled though the pages.

"God is good! I just knew they would work until they got some leads on who did this to your sister. It won't be long before they catch the heathen and bring him to justice" she smirked and glanced in my direction.

I bit my bottom lip and shook my head to let this bitch know that if she uttered another word it would be a dirt nap for her ass. Adrian was so engrossed in what he was doing that the looks we exchanged went unnoticed.

"It's crazy that they are saying the killer could be a man or a woman" said Falynn.

"That's right" Adrian responded "And these boot prints and fibers will hopefully be a key piece in solving this mystery."

"I overheard you say that it were a woman she would wear a size 12. That's a big ass foot for a lady. It shouldn't be that hard finding out who had boots in that size" she said looking down at my feet.

Thank God Adrian hadn't picked up on the hints she was throwing. At this point I had begun hyperventilating and had to sneak away to the bathroom and gain my composure.

My hands were sweating and shaking, my heart was racing and I felt like I was going to faint. I was having a full blown anxiety attack. This bitch had to go! Especially if she was going to try and be slick and throw signs to Adrian. Besides how could I be sure she would keep her mouth shut even with the money she was about to receive. And that was another issue in itself. Where the hell was I supposed to get my hands on that type of loot? I had to find a way to shut this bitch up without hurting the baby. I knew it was only a matter of time before she would spill everything. And I had to make sure that never happened. This bitch was truly deranged if she thought she was going to take my family from me. There was no getting around it, I had to move quickly.

I reached down and pulled out the brown paper bag that I kept hidden underneath the bathroom sink. After seating myself on the toilet I breathed in and out of the bag slowly before bending over and placing my head between my knees. When I was finally calm enough and the feeling of faint had passed I patted my face with a cool rag and popped a valium before emerging back into the kitchen only to find out that Adrian and Falynn had left the room and were chilling in the family room. Just as I expected his black ass was rubbing her belly. Oh well, that was the least of my worries at the moment.

When we finally went to bed that night Adrian still had an attitude. He went on and on about how I wasn't supportive of his efforts. I hate to say it but he was right. And as much as I tried to hide it, my displeasure still managed to work its way to the surface. And to add insult to injury he had the nerve to say that it was a shame that a stranger seemed to be more in his corner when it came to finding Tasha's killer than I was.

Falynn was as fake as the day was long and low and behold this bitch had successfully pulled the wool over my man's eyes with her fake ass concern. I can't stand people who pretend to be something that they are not. I couldn't wait to expose her lying ass but for now I needed to get some rest. It had been a long ass day and I was worn out. I tried to snuggle up next to Adrian but he scooted all the way on the other side of the bed and turned his back to me.

Just as I was about to doze off my phone vibrated on the nightstand. I quickly rejected the call and looked to see who it was. It was that damn Dr Johnson. I glanced over to see if Adrian was still sleeping before creeping out of bed and taking the phone with me.

It was after midnight and he was still blowing up my phone. His crazy ass just wouldn't take no for an answer. "I'm about to cuss this mutha fucka out!" I said as I went into the kitchen to make sure I wouldn't wake anyone up. Just as I was about to dial his number the phone rang again. It was him!

"What the hell is wrong with you calling me at this hour?" I kept my voice at a loud whisper but I really wanted to scream.

"I'm sorry but I need you Wolverine. I've been going crazy all day thinking about you putting the iron fist on me."

I was about to hang up in this nigga's face when he told me he was outside.

"What the fuck? Have you lost your damn mind?"

"Hell yeah I done lost it. I'm crazy for you."

I rushed over and peeped out of the window to see the doc's car parked two doors down on the opposite side of the street. "How long have you been out there?" I was mad as hell. As if I didn't have enough on my plate already, now I had to deal with this freak lunatic.

"I just got here."

"Well you need to leave NOW! And don't ever come here again."

"Fuck that! I need you now Flipper! And if you don't come out to the car I'm coming to the door!" he yelled out of desperation.

"Alright dammit! I'm on the way out, just stay there."

"Imma kill this son of a bitch! He done clocked all the way out with this damn hand obsession of his" I fumed as I grabbed my robe off of the back of the hook on the bathroom door, wrapped it around me and quietly tipped out of the side door. I made sure I turned off the flood lights so I wouldn't draw any extra attention to myself.

I already had my mind made up; when I got in this car I was gonna cuss his ass into oblivion, however when I opened the car door nothing could have prepared me for the sight that was in front of me. I had to do a double take because I thought my eyes were playing tricks on me.

"You crazy bastard! Don't be rolling up on my house... what the hell?"

The Dr. was sitting in the driver's seat wearing a tight ass velour track suit that looked like it was from 1985. He had the jacket unzipped so low that it not only showed the taco meat on his chest but his big ass belly as well, which by the way it looked like he had greased up. And what the fuck was that on his head? This fool had the nerve to have a straight, Ike Turner mushroom wiglet on.

Despite all the messiness that had took place that day and the fact that he was actually at my house I couldn't help but laugh out loud. As much as I hated to admit it, it was the first time I had laughed all day and it actually felt pretty good.

"Doc what the hell you got on your head?" I asked as I let out a hearty laugh.

I was hysterical but he was dead serious. "You like it baby? I wore it just for you" he announced proudly as he straightened his bangs in the rearview mirror.

As much as I hoped that this was joke, this man was as serious as a heart attack. I didn't want to laugh in the man's face but he looked like a damn fool.

"Hell naw! Your crazy ass is giving me The Beatles meets Precious."

The Doc just waved his hand at my comment and straightened his collar. "Hush girl, I pulled this out of my special occasion stash."

"And speaking of crazy, why are you here? I told you I was busy today and you just keep calling over and over like a damn mad man. This shit has to stop today Doc. I know we have an agreement and all but you can't be blowing up my spot."

Just that quick the tone in my voice had changed. The humor was short lived seeing as this was the major reason we were even sitting in the car talking. There was no telling who could be watching us. Thank God Adrian and that damn Falynn were fast asleep.

"I'm sorry baby but I just been think about them phalanges of yours all day long. I'm like a damn dope fiend when it comes to your claws. I'm like Pookie in New Jack City, they be calling me," he cooed reaching for my hands that I quickly snatched away.

"Phalanges? What the fuck is a phalange?"

The Doc grinned and sat straight up in his seat as though he was taking pride in giving me the clinical answer. "That's the medical term for the bones in your hands and feet baby."

"Well call my shit hands. I done had about enough of all these damn stupid ass nick names your freaky ass keeps coming up with."

"I'm sorry baby but you just have some of the most gorgeous big hands that I ever laid eyes on" he responded as he gently reached over and once again and took my hand to caress it. He immediately noticed the cut on two of the knuckles from where I had punched the TV screen earlier that day.

"What the hell? Who did this to you hoofy? I mean Pebbles…."

"Nobody, I had an accident" I responded as I tried unsuccessfully to pull away from the tight grip he had on my wrist.

"An accident? Lemme see," he replied as he examined my hand front and back.

"Did Adrian do this to you? You ain't trying to cover for his ass are you? Cause I will bust a cap in that muthafucka for my woman," he said mean mugging the house from the side view mirror. "Don't let the Dr. in front of my name fool you. I use to have a little gangster in me back in the day."

"Your woman? Sigh… look Doc I told you I had an accident. Adrian didn't touch me. And imma just keep it real with you. You need to get some help with that fetish of yours. This shit has gotten out of control," I grunted, finally breaking free from his grip.

"I know… it's just that well…. I feel like I'm falling in love with you Pebbles. I know I was wrong for showing up at your house like this and I won't ever do it again. I just couldn't help it. I would do anything for you to be my woman Pebbles. That nigga Adrian just don't know how good he got it. I wore all this for you 'cause I know y'all young girls like niggas who be clean. You always seeing me in my work clothes and I wanted to let you know how a nigga like me roll outside the office. I wanted you to see my swag. Hell I even put my gold slice in for you." With that he turned facing me grinning so that his gold cap on his tooth was glistening in the street light.

"Ohhh yeahh….. I see." It took everything in me not to bust out laughing again. However as bizarre as it sounded the crazy ass Doc seemed to be in my corner and despite the fact that I had turned his ass out he was actually becoming a friend.

"Look Doc. I already have a man. Adrian and I are happy. I appreciate the offer and everything that you are doing for me but I'm already spoken for."

I felt kinda bad breaking the old geezer's heart but it had to be done. I had to be firm with him so we could get back to business without any distractions.

"I understand, I just thought I had finally found the real deal. A brotha' like me gets lonely sometimes ya know? I just want you to know what I feel for you is real girl. And I ain't never gon' give up on you, on us…." with that the doc wiped a tear from his eye.

After finally talking him down from trying to whoop Adrian's ass over my hand and convincing him that we could never be an item I was able to get him to leave quietly without making a scene. Once he was gone I slid back in bed and fell asleep damn near as soon as my head hit the pillow. What a day!

Canine Loaf

The next few weeks went by with me trying to appease Falynn. Every time a thought came across her mind about something she wanted to eat her big ass summonsed me to fix it. Besides cooking she had me keeping her room clean, doing her laundry, and even running her errands. This shit had to stop.

I still hadn't figured out how I was gonna get rid of her ass once the baby was born. Because there was no way in hell I was letting this hoe get away with the shit she was pulling. Hell I was tired as hell waiting on this bitch, especially after a hard day's work. Shit I'm supposed to be laid up living the good life with my husband. I'm the one that should be getting all the pampering and this bitch got me waiting on her ass hand and foot.

The only positive thing that was coming out of this whole thing was the fact that Adrian had finally forgiven me for being so insensitive when it came to his news about Tasha's killer. And he was also pleased to see that I was being so attentive to Falynn. His dumb ass actually thought we were becoming friends. Little did he know we were the worst of enemies.

I decided to use a few vacation days to get some rest and to try and get my head together. After I saw Adrian off to work I laid back down to relax and watch a little TV before I hit up the grocery store. The princess wanted a meatloaf today and I had to run and grab all the ingredients.

As I was flipping through the channels I landed on Good Times. I always loved that show when I was coming up and I tried to catch the reruns whenever I could. This just so happened to be the episode where Florida and James's friend made them a meatloaf and they were afraid to eat it because they found out that she had been eating dog food. Not only was the episode hilarious even though I had seen it many times. It also gave me an idea. If this heffa wanted a meatloaf I was gonna make her a REAL good one. "I'm putting dog food in that shit," I said to myself.

For a split second I contemplated on how crazy it sounded and the effects that it may have on the baby, but I figured as long as I read the ingredients on the can and there were no additives I would be straight. I didn't have one ounce of guilt about what I was about to do considering the fact that this trick was making my life a living hell. Besides it wasn't any worse than me spitting in her shit every chance I got. Oh yes this bitch was getting some Alpo today! I was so excited about my plan that I immediately jumped up and got dressed. This was the first time in months that I felt like I was in control of my life again and it felt wonderful. I was on an absolute high thinking about her savoring every bite. When I was finished with her ass she would be barking like the dog she was.

As I went up and down the pet food isle I took time to read the labels on the cans carefully to make sure the food was as natural as possible. I mean just because I'm making this bitch a canine loaf didn't mean wanted my child having any side effects from all the added chemicals. After all, I didn't want his little ass coming out growling and shit.

I finally settled a brand that had 60% horse meat and the rest was beef, lamb, and chicken. "Hmmm they say horse is supposed to be lean meat," I said to justify my purchase as I tossed several cans into the buggy.

"What kind of dog do you have?"

"Huh?" I jumped and turned around to see a little old white lady standing next to me struggling to reach a can on the top shelf.

"I'm sorry, I didn't mean to startle you dear," she said, smiling at me with a wrinkly grin before thanking me for grabbing the can for her.

"Thank you dear. I have a Scottish Terrier, what kind of dog do you have?"

"You know I really don't know. It's a mutt."

"Well mutts need to eat good too," she laughed glancing at all the cans of food in the buggy.

I laughed and nodded.

"Lemme ask you something. Are you a dog lover?"

"Why yes! I love animals."

"I see… well the thing is I have this new dog and she's extremely noisy. How do you shut a dog up?" I asked.

The old lady chuckled before giving her advice.

"I'm not really sure dear, but I hear you can spray them with a water bottle each time they start barking for just no reason. That's supposed to train them to be quiet."

"Thanks! I'm gonna try that!"

"You quite welcome, have a nice day."

"Damn that was a close call," I said to myself before hitting up the spice isle then grabbing a few cans of tomato paste and some mixed veggies. Ms. Falynn was about to have a real good dinner tonight.

Once I got back home I quickly went to work removing the food from the cans and putting it in a plastic container that I hid in the bottom of the fridge till I was ready to use it. I didn't have time to mix up the meatloaf just yet because I had to dispose of the cans before miss nosey ass came out and caught me. I hopped back the car and dropped off the bag of cans to the same dumpster that I had put the busted TV in a few weeks ago. I couldn't have made my move a moment too soon. As soon as I walked in the door Falynn was standing there looking out of the living room window.

"Where the hell you been?" she sneered suspiciously.

"None of your damn business" I snapped back as I walked past her like she didn't exist.

"Oh it's my business, whether you want to believe it or not. I thought I heard you come in from the store a few minutes ago. Where did you sneak back out too?" she asked as she proceeded to follow me around the house.

This bitch was really testing me today. I should have picked up that damn water bottle.

"Let's get something straight right now. I don't answer to you or no damn body else for that matter. And I suggest you stop sticking your damn nose where it don't belong."

She giggled to herself as she grabbed an apple out of the fruit bowl and handed it to me.

I snatched it out of her hand and rinsed it off.

"I want that peeled and cut up also" she demanded as I was about to hand it back to her.

I smiled to myself and kept my peace. I was actually laughing inside knowing what I had in store for her ass later on.

"Oh you don't have to answer to nobody huh? Maybe Adrian would be interested in knowing you snuck your ass out the other night to sit in the car with that nigga. I'll bet your ass will have to answer to that," she said as she smirked and took the apple from me. "Who was that? You creeping on Adrian?"

This hoe wasn't sleep after all. "Her ass don't miss shit!" I thought.

I didn't say a single word. I wasn't going to give her the satisfaction of getting a rise out of me today. Instead I headed back to my room with her following close behind me.

"Fine go ahead and ignore me, but your ass just betta' make sure you got the stuff to make my meatloaf with."

I slammed the door in her face and stayed in my room till I thought she was taking a nap. That's pretty much all her fat ass did these days was sleep. And that was fine with me. Not only did I need a break from her running her damn mouth, I needed to mix up my special recipe without any interruptions.

Once I was back in the kitchen I turned the oven on 350 to preheat it and started grabbing my ingredients. I didn't have any idea how this damn dog food was going to hold up in the oven so I decided to mix in a pinch of ground beef. However, the ration was very small compared to the amount of dog food. I didn't want that bitch getting a treat. I wanted to make sure her ass was eating damn near three cans of dog food. After I mixed the dog food with the hamburger I added in some diced onions and bell peppers, some breadcrumbs and an egg to hold it together, some diced tomatoes, Lawry's and a ton of other seasonings to mask the flavor and the smell. When it was finally formed I poured a can of tomato sauce over the whole thing, wrapped the pan in foil and placed it in the oven. My only fear was that the shit would start smelling weird and give it away.

While it was cooking I peeled some potatoes to mash and made some corn bread. Before I knew it the aroma from all spices and herbs started to light up house. And much to my surprise it smelled delicious! I almost slipped up and tasted it my damn self till I remembered what it had in it. Curiosity didn't kill this cat!

Just as I was putting some butter in the mixed vegetables Falynn emerged from her room.

"Something smells good as hell! Is that the meatloaf?" she asked as she took a seat at the counter with her mouthwatering.

"Yeah that's the meatloaf," I responded rolling my eyes.

"I'm hungry as hell, gimme a piece now!" she exclaimed as I pulled it from the oven and vented the foil letting the steam and more of the rich aroma escape.

"You don't wanna wait till the veggies are done?"

"Hell naw, there's nothing like meatloaf hot out of the oven."

I fixed her a plate with a big slice of the canine loaf and a heaping spoon of mashed potatoes. I then poured her up a glass of sweet tea and waited.

I damn near jumped for joy when I watched her scarf it down so fast that she almost choked. She finally came up for air and took a sip of tea after her plate was clean.

"Man I gotta give it to you, I can't stand your ass but you can burn. That was the best meatloaf I done had in a long time. You ain't eating none?" she asked.

"Naw I'm not in the mood. I lost my appetite for it seeing as I had to slave over a damn hot ass stove all day," I responded giving her the side eye so as to not arouse her suspicion.

"Oh well that just means more for me! Ain't nothing like leftover meatloaf sandwiches. Hit me with another slice!" she said as she slid her plate towards me for seconds.

When she finally had her fill she patted her stuffed belly, belched and headed back to her room.

"Damn that was good; a bitch got the itis after that good ass meal. Nigga you alright with me today."

"Glad you enjoyed it…"

"*Mmm hmmm, mace me will ya? Pebbles will always have the last laugh,*" I thought. I had finally started getting this bitch back and it felt divine.

When Adrian got in that evening it was all I could do to hold him back from tasting the meatloaf. I had made us our own dinner of baked chicken and wild rice but he wasn't trying to hear it. The smell hit him when he walked in the door and drew him in.

"Damn bae what's smelling so good up in here?"

"I cooked dinner for us. I baked some chicken and made some wild rice."

"Nah, I smell something else. Is that meatloaf?" he asked as he walked into the kitchen. "It is meatloaf. Why did you make two meals?" he asked as he washed his hands in the kitchen sink.

"I made the meatloaf for Falynn, it was a special request."

"Well I'm damn sure 'bout to sample it," he said as he reached for a saucer and proceeded to spoon himself up a slice.

"No! I mean… don't eat that. I made that especially for her. She was craving it." I tried to stop him but he gently nudged me to the side.

"Damn girl look at you. All protective over Falynn's meal and shit," he laughed before getting serious. "And speaking of Falynn I've been meaning to tell you that it's really sweet how you have been taking care of her the past few weeks. We got off to a little rocky start but it seems like y'all are really bonding now."

"Yeah well I figured I should try and make up for the attitude I had been having towards her seeing as she is carrying our child. Plus it's not her fault that I was experiencing my own insecurities. I wanted to do something extra special for her. That why I cooked this meal today for her, not for you," I griped as I made another grab for the plate. I couldn't let my man eat this shit.

Adrian laughed and playfully dodged me. "I know it's for her but she's giving some of this meatloaf up today. It smells too damn good. Besides she can't eat the whole thing by herself anyway." With that he took a huge bite in his mouth. I thought I was going to throw up right there in the kitchen! Just the thought of how much dog food I had put in that shit made me gag. His eyes rolled back as he smacked his lips and dug in for a few more bites before speaking.

"Damn you done out did yourself today bae. This is delicious. You should have made this meal for us. Come here and gimme some sugar."

"*What the hell?*" I thought. I didn't want to kiss this nigga. It was bad enough I couldn't stop him from eating the damn meatloaf. I'll be damned if I was gonna taste it too.

Upon my hesitation Adrian leaned over a planted a huge wet kiss on my lips. I recoiled in disgust as I tasted the sauce on his lips.

"I'm so proud of you bae."

"Thanks baby…"

I couldn't get to the bathroom fast enough when I though he wasn't watching. I had to brush my teeth and rinse with some mouthwash. Fuck it… I guess the whole family tasted the canine loaf today.

Dear Momma

They say no matter how old you are you still want your momma when you are hurting. And that's exactly what I wanted right now. I missed my family so much that words couldn't even express it. In my quest to chase after, and successfully get my man I had totally alienated them. Even though I had talked to my mother a few days ago it still wasn't like seeing her beautiful face. Momma always had a way of making everything better.

My life was truly fucked up at this point. Even though I had gotten my man I had spun a web of lies so big that I felt like I was never gonna find my way out. Not to mention, this bitch Falynn; she had worked her way into our lives and threatened to destroy everything that I had worked so hard to build. There was no getting around the fact that I was going to have to take care of her, permanently. And not only didn't I have any idea of how I was going to dispose of her ass. I was now faced with the cold hard reality that I was about to become a serial killer if I stayed on the track that I was on.

Tasha's death ate away at me a little each day. Yet I went about with my daily routine without a grain of remorse each time I thought about her exposing me to Adrian. I was torn between the love of my best friend and the love of my man. And in the end Adrian won. He always won….

As I sat in the car in the parking garage after work that day reflecting over all that I had been through the past few years I began to cry. I wanted to pull off and drive home but something hit me. I suddenly felt like I was losing my mind. I had been lying to my parents for so long that I didn't even know the truth anymore. Despite the fact that momma or anyone else in my family hadn't seen me in years she still never gave up on me. She still begged for me to visit each time we spoke. Luckily I had given her false addresses a few times or she would have been dead on my trail. My momma was determined to find her baby, with or without the help of my father who thought I was a lost cause. She set out a few times on her own to look for me and each time I had to throw her off by telling her I was traveling for work. I was a mess.

"I want my mommy" I sobbed uncontrollably as held myself and rocked back and forth sucking my thumb. I was losing it. "Momma! I need you momma! Come hold your baby momma!"

I thought about how I lied and deceived one of the few people in this world who loved me unconditionally and it made my heart bleed. When I finally pulled myself together I blew my nose and pulled off.

I ended up at the liquor store around the block from my house. I went in and bought a half pint of vodka, came back to the car and slammed it straight.

"Get yourself together bitch!" I said as I looked at my disheveled reflection in the rearview mirror.

I wiped the tears from my eyes and decided that I would call my momma and tell her about the sex change. Somehow I felt like even though I was lying to her about everything else this would still lift a huge burden off of me and her. I had no idea if I was going to get away with the shit I was about to do to Falynn and in the event that I didn't at least I would feel like I had made some kind of peace with my parents.

I didn't know what the odds were of getting away with murder a second time but if I did in fact get away it would be a beautiful thing. I would tell momma the truth about the fact that Adrian didn't know I use to be a man and I'm sure she would understand. And daddy… well he would come around soon enough. We could all be one big happy family, like it was supposed to be. My mother could meet her son in law (whom she already knew) and her new grandbaby. And little AJ could bond with his grandparents.

"Yeah… that's how it's supposed to be," I said smiling at myself in the mirror.

"Imma call momma and everything is going to be ok." I said as I dialed her number.

I felt my palms once again getting sweaty as the phone rang on the other end of the line. I had never been nervous when I talked to my momma but this time was different. I was about to tell her the truth, well at least part of it and that counted for something.

"Hello"

"Hey... it's me."

"Hello baby, it's so good to hear your voice."

"Hey momma, how are you?"

"I'm good baby. The question is how are you? I wasn't expecting to hear from you again this soon."

My heart sank when she said those words. I didn't talk to her as nearly as much as I needed too.

"I'm sorry momma," I responded softly as tears once again began to fall.

"What is it baby?" she asked, becoming immediately concerned. "Are you in some kind trouble?"

"No it's not that…."

"Well what is it then? I can hear it in your voice. Did somebody hurt my baby?"

"Momma….I need to tell you something…..I'm a woman."

"Awww baby is that what this is all about? I know you have always said that you felt like you were a woman. And that you were in the wrong body. I'm sorry we didn't get the surgery you wanted when you asked us but we just couldn't afford it. And you know how your daddy and I feel about the lifestyle seeing as we are Christian and all but that hasn't made us love you any less," she reassured. "I just wish you would stop running long enough for us to be a family again. I miss you so much Peyton."

"I miss y'all too momma. And you right I'm tired of running. I just wanted to call you and tell you the truth."

"The truth?" she asked, sounding confused.

"Yes the truth, I'm REALLY a woman momma. I had the sex reassignment surgery a few years ago and I've been running from y'all ever since to keep it a secret. I'm so sorry for all that I put y'all through. I really do love you and daddy. I miss my lil bro and sis also."

"So that's it!" Momma exclaimed, sounding as if she were having an Ahh haa moment.

"Huh? What you talking about momma?" I sniffled.

"Chile my spirit don't lead me wrong. I knew it was something different about you. It has been for a while now, especially your voice. I just prayed day and night that you weren't still on that stuff and running them streets. I thought you had got mixed up with some folks that had you doing God knows what and I was worried sick about you, especially after losing your friend Tasha. That was so awful what happened to that poor girl."

"Yeah…. It was awful. I miss her so much."

"I know you do baby."

"So you not mad that I didn't tell you about the sex change?"

"Let me ask you this; are YOU happy with your decision?"

"Ohhh yes momma! I'm the happiest I've ever in my life been since becoming a woman. And you should know that I was never on drugs momma. Yes I was running the streets and hoeing for the money I needed for the operation but I was never strung out. I done cleaned up my act, got a respectable job and even got married momma.

"Then chile a sex change is the the least of my worries. Especially since I now know why you been running from us all this time and acting so strange. As long as you are happy and safe that's all that matters. I hope you finally found the peace of mind you been searching for baby."

I stared into the distance as I listened to her words and thought about how I was going to kill Falynn.

"I don't have complete peace yet, but it's coming real soon. Oh and guess what? You and daddy 'bout to be grandparents."

Momma was overcome with joy. "Lawd chile you done made my day. I'm so happy for you baby. I can't wait to see you and my new grandchild and son in law.

"I can't wait either. Momma… what about daddy and the rest of the family."

"Hush chile, you let me take care of ya daddy. And everybody else gon' have to get in where they fit in."

I busted out laughing. "Momma, what you know about that phrase?"

"What? You think I'm too old to be hip?"

"No I don't… not at all. I love you momma."

"I love you too Pey… Oh yeah I almost forgot to ask. What's your name now baby?"

"My name is Pebbles."

"I love you too Pebbles."

So that was it. I had finally come clean to momma about my lifestyle. And for tiny that moment in time everything was alright in my world. It didn't even matter that I had to take another life. I had already offed my best friend whom I loved dearly, so killing Falynn would be a breeze. Hell I don't even like this hoe. I killed once and I'm not above killing again. If I snuffed the life of my best friend in the whole world in the name of love, what the hell does this bitch think I would do to the average muthafucka that tried to stand in the way of my happy family? And as far as I was concerned she was already dead to me. I just needed to make that shit a reality.....

The End

Midnite Love

53510845R00066

Made in the USA
Lexington, KY
07 July 2016